DIALOGUES OF THE DEAD

ADAPTED FROM THE DIALOGUES OF LUCIAN

BAUDELAIRE JONES

Black Box Press
Los Angeles

Inquiries concerning amateur and professional performing rights should be addressed to the author at: jones@theatredatabase.com

ISBN 978-0-6151-5013-0

First Edition

AUTHOR'S NOTE

In adapting *Dialogues of the Dead*, I have made every attempt to remain true to the original spirit of Lucian's dialogues. The spirit—not the details. If you're a student, reading this adaptation for a class assignment, find another translation! Quick! If you read this book, YOU WILL FAIL! Not only have I updated many antiquated cultural references to modern equivalents that the average reader can more easily understand, but I've also gone so far as to recast several of Lucian's original characters with more modern counterparts—most notably: Howard Hughes, John D. Rockefeller, Anna Nicole Smith, Clarence Darrow, Sigmund Freud, Michael Moore, Saddam Hussein, and Jack the Ripper. The upside—this makes the text infinitely more readable. The downside—it may result in some confusing classroom discussions. Peace. And enjoy.

—BAUDELAIRE JONES

DIALOGUES OF THE DEAD

I

[DIOGENES. POLLUX.]

DIOGENES: Pollux! Wait up!

POLLUX: Diogenes—what's wrong?

DIOGENES: Nothing. I have a job for you.

POLLUX: A job?

DIOGENES: Yeah.

POLLUX: I'm sort of busy.

DIOGENES: It's nothing, really—won't take a minute.

POLLUX: What is it?

DIOGENES: Next time you go up—

POLLUX: To earth?

DIOGENES: It's your turn tomorrow, isn't it?

POLLUX: I'll have to check the schedule, but—

DIOGENES: Well, if you come across Michael Moore, the filmmaker—he's usually hanging around the Capital, throwing eggs at congressmen, or boating 9/11 rescue workers to Cuba for free health care—can you give him a message for me?

POLLUX: What message?

DIOGENES: Tell him—if mortal subjects cease to provide sufficient laughter, Diogenes invites him to come below and find a richer vein of material for his amusement.

POLLUX: You want the man to kill himself for a few laughs?

DIOGENES: Oh, you don't understand! Michael would do anything for a good laugh! He's a real prankster! The problem is, on earth, there's always a bit of uncertainty, you know—one can never really be sure about the afterlife, and that dulls the joke. Here, he can laugh with security—like me. Tell him what fun it is to see millionaires, politicians, dictators, even Hollywood actors—all reduced to the same size as the rest of us. Tell him how they pout and cry and go on and on about how important they used to be! He won't be able to resist!

POLLUX: All right, I'll tell him. What does he look like?

DIOGENES: Fat white guy. Wears glasses—usually a baseball cap. Just look for outraged conservatives. Whoever they're pointing at— that's him. He's always laughing and playing some sort of practical joke on the most hypocritical old fart he can find—and he's always trying to catch it on film. Makes documentaries. Very philosophical. Even won an Academy Award. That reminds me—can I give you one other message?

POLLUX: Go ahead.

DIOGENES: Tell all the philosophers up there to stop being so ridiculous, arguing over metaphysics, and trying to trick each other with horn and crocodile puzzles—and that damn Rubik's cube—it's such a waste of time!

POLLUX: You know if I criticize them they'll just use a bunch of big words and make me look like a fool.

DIOGENES: What do you care? Tell them to go to hell!

POLLUX: Fine. Anything else?

DIOGENES: Yes! Tell the rich stockbrokers, investment bankers, real estate tycoons—Donald Trump, Warren Buffett, that sort—

POLLUX: You know Buffett just gave away something like 30 billion dollars to charity?

DIOGENES: Good for him. That leaves how many billion?

POLLUX: You were saying?

DIOGENES: Tell them to stop hoarding money. What's the point? I mean, why spend every waking moment multiplying dollars when, next thing you know, you're dead and don't need anything more than a penny for crossing into the underworld?

POLLUX: Stop hoarding. Got it.

DIOGENES: Oh! One more thing! A word to the pretty boys and athletes—Johnny Depp, Michael Vick, and that wrestler—what's his name? He does that *look* …

POLLUX: What look?

DIOGENES: You know.
              [*DIOGENES makes a face, his eyes bulging.*]

POLLUX: The Rock?

DIOGENES: The Rock! Tell him, and all the rest, that pretty eyes, long hair, and bulging muscles won't do them any good here. Tell them any two men look just the same when you peel them down to the bone.

POLLUX: I hope that's it—I can't remember any more messages.

DIOGENES: Just one more. Tell the Americans to lighten up. There's more to life than making war and building empires! Didn't they learn anything from the Romans? And don't get me started on that President of theirs—

POLLUX: Oh, no—that's going too far! Your other commissions I will execute, but I'm not going near that man—he's crazy!

DIOGENES: Fine. Let him off the hook then, if it's such a big deal, but tell all the others what I said.

* * *

II

*[MIDAS, JOHN D. ROCKEFELLER, HOWARD
HUGHES, and MICHAEL MOORE stand before
the throne of PLUTO. MICHAEL MOORE wears
a baseball cap and carries a video camera on his
shoulder—he is filming the others.]*

MIDAS: It's completely unacceptable!

JOHN D. ROCKEFELLER: He's ruining the neighborhood!

HOWARD HUGHES: Either you transfer him to other quarters, or
you're going to have a mass migration on your hands!

PLUTO: What's this all about, Michael?

MICHAEL MOORE: Ask them.

PLUTO: Well? What harm has he done to your ghostly community?

HOWARD HUGHES: What harm? He mocks us constantly! Midas
here, and Rockefeller and I, we can't even reminisce about the good
old days of wealth and luxury without him laughing and calling us
rude names—"slaves" and "garbage," he says!

MIDAS: And that camera! He catches every little thing we say, and
then plays it back over and over—

JOHN D. ROCKEFELLER: Don't forget the singing!

HOWARD HUGHES: Yes! He sings constantly!

JOHN D. ROCKEFELLER: And he isn't any good!

MIDAS: He sucks!

JOHN D. ROCKEFELLER: He's worse than that kid …

MIDAS: Which one?

JOHN D. ROCKEFELLER: On *American Idol*—what's his name?

MIDAS: Sanjaya?

JOHN D. ROCKEFELLER: Ugggh!

HOWARD HUGHES: The point is—he's a nuisance!

PLUTO: Michael, is this true?

MICHAEL MOORE: Sure—every bit of it. I hate these fuckers. It's not enough that they got to lord it over the rest of us during life, now they want to harp on it for the rest of eternity. It's my mission to annoy them until they shut the fuck up.

PLUTO: Yes, but … you have to understand—they've suffered terrible losses. It may take them a while to adjust.

MICHAEL MOORE: Pluto! Are you kidding me?! You're really gonna take their side?!

PLUTO: I'm not taking any side, but I won't tolerate quarrelling down here.

MICHAEL MOORE: Listen up, you rich scumbags—I don't care what he says—I won't quit hounding you until you stop putting on airs.

PLUTO: Michael—

MICHAEL MOORE: Wherever you go, I'll be right behind you— laughing, filming, singing you down!

HOWARD HUGHES: Presumptuous ass!

MICHAEL MOORE: No—*you're* the presumptuous ones—when you expect better men than you to fall down at your feet, when you trample all over liberty and justice, when you steal from those who have less than you! Only you forgot one thing—you forgot about death! Now it's payback time! Now comes the weeping and gnashing of teeth! Everything you had—everything you treasured—it's gone! All gone! Bye-bye!

HOWARD HUGHES: He's right!

MIDAS: It's lost!

JOHN D. ROCKEFELLER: Oh, God!

MIDAS: My gold—

JOHN D. ROCKEFELLER: My oil—

HOWARD HUGHES: My beauties—

MICHAEL MOORE: That's it! Let it all out! You do the whining, and I'll chime in with a Hallelujah chorus! Smile for the camera, boys—here we go!

* * *

III

*[MUHAMMAD and JESUS sit praying. Enter
MICHAEL MOORE, his camera still rolling.]*

MICHAEL MOORE: Well, well, well—what do we have here?!
Muhammad and Jesus! What a pair! Mind if I join you?

JESUS: Suit yourself.

MICHAEL MOORE: I'm a little surprised to find the two of you
together.

MUHAMMAD: It isn't by choice, believe me.

MICHAEL MOORE: What do you mean?

MUHAMMAD: These quarters were assigned.

MICHAEL MOORE: Ah, I see—some sort of punishment. But what
are you guys doing here at all—shouldn't you be up there somewhere,
drinking ambrosia and partying with the gods? I mean, what are you
doing down here with us mortals—in the underworld?

JESUS: Isn't it obvious?

MICHAEL MOORE: But … Hades is for men—not gods.

MUHAMMAD: I never claimed divinity. I was merely a prophet.

MICHAEL MOORE: Right—you only *spoke* to gods. Still, you'd
think they could've pulled some strings for you. And all those
temples built in your honor—doesn't that count for something?

MUHAMMAD: We cannot control what happens after our lifetimes.
If men want to build temples, they'll build temples.

MICHAEL MOORE: Yeah, but … you must have done something to sort of encourage it—right? I mean, when you were alive?
> *[MUHAMMAD shrugs. MOORE turns his camera to JESUS.]*

What about you—if you're down here … are you telling me the whole virgin birth thing was a hoax?

JESUS: I wouldn't call it a hoax exactly.

MUHAMMAD: Complete hoax.

JESUS: Shut up, Muhammad.

MICHAEL MOORE: What *would* you call it? If it's not a hoax—

JESUS: Look, I'm not ashamed of anything I said or did up there. I had my reasons.

MICHAEL MOORE: Like what?

JESUS: I took a violent religion, based on fear and a vengeful God, and I transformed it into a gospel of love and peace. "Turn the other cheek," "Love your neighbor as yourself"—that's all me.

MUHAMMAD: Love of the world is the root of all evil.

JESUS: What's that supposed to mean?

MUHAMMAD: Nothing—I'm just saying.

JESUS: You're *always* saying.

MICHAEL MOORE: But … you said you were a god!

JESUS: You think anyone was gonna listen to a carpenter's son?

MICHAEL MOORE: So you lied to get attention?

MUHAMMAD: Lied his ass off.

JESUS: I made the world a better place.

MICHAEL MOORE: Did you?

JESUS: I think so.

MICHAEL MOORE: But … do you realize how many wars have been fought in your name—both of you? How many people have died arguing over your dogma? How many innocent people have been killed?

JESUS: Can you imagine how many wars would've been fought if I hadn't come—if I hadn't done away with that vengeful God—how many *more* people would have died?

MUHAMMAD: If you hadn't perverted the religion, I wouldn't have had to restore it.

JESUS: I didn't pervert it! You perverted it!

MUHAMMAD: Say that to my face!

MICHAEL MOORE: Okay, okay—I can see we're not going to agree here. One more thing, though. If you could tell the folks back home one thing—what would it be?

JESUS: Love one another.

MUHAMMAD: Jihad, baby.

MICHAEL MOORE: *[To JESUS.]* By the way … off the record … is it true what they say about you and Mary Magdalene?

JESUS: No comment.

* * *

IV

[HERMES and CHARON stand on the shore of the river Styx. CHARON tends to his boat.]

HERMES: Ferryman, what do you say we settle up? That way we can avoid any confusion later on.

CHARON: Fine with me, Hermes. What have you got?

HERMES: There was that anchor—two hundred bucks.

CHARON: Two hundred bucks?! For an anchor?!

HERMES: That's what it cost me.

CHARON: If you say so.

HERMES: I do.

CHARON: All right, then—what else?

HERMES: One rowlock-strap—forty dollars.

CHARON: Two-forty—got it.

HERMES: Then there was that needle—for mending the sail. Caulking-wax. Nails. And cord for the brace.

CHARON: How much?

HERMES: Another forty for the lot.

CHARON: Well worth the money.

HERMES: That's it—unless I've forgotten something.

CHARON: Two-eighty then.

HERMES: When can you pay?

CHARON: Good question.

HERMES: What's that supposed to mean?

CHARON: Right now I'm dead broke. But we'll have another war or plague soon enough, and the passengers will start piling up—penny a fare, I should be able to pay you back in no time.

HERMES: So I have to wait for some sort of catastrophe if I want to get paid?

CHARON: What you gonna do? Not much business right now—the peace, you know.

HERMES: Peace! Pfff! Do you remember the old days, Charon—when men were men? The state they used to come down in! All blood and guts! The wounds of battle! Nowadays, a man is poisoned by his wife, or gets diabetes from overeating—a pale, spiritless lot—nothing like the men of old! Although … there are still a few who meet a violent end … usually they owe somebody *money*.

CHARON: Is that some kind of threat?

HERMES: Maybe.

* * *

V

[PLUTO. HERMES.]

PLUTO: You remember that old fart—J. Howard Marshall?

HERMES: The name rings a bell …

PLUTO: Oil tycoon—married Anna Nicole Smith.

HERMES: The Playmate! Sure! The one with the really big—

PLUTO: That's her.

HERMES: Yeah! She's really something!

PLUTO: He was worth billions.

HERMES: I remember that. The guy was like a walking corpse. He was what—ninety?

PLUTO: Eighty-nine.

HERMES: Yeah, she married him for his money, but he pulled a fast one or something.

PLUTO: He transferred his entire estate to one of his sons before the marriage. She didn't know, of course.

HERMES: That's dirty pool, if you ask me.

PLUTO: It's his money! Why shouldn't he protect it?! He's supposed to hand over his entire fortune to some brainless bimbo?!

HERMES: If he didn't want to share, he shouldn't have married her. C'mon, Pluto—it's not like the old goat didn't get something out of the deal. I mean, the guy's got one foot in the grave, and he gets a nice young piece of—

PLUTO: A few hand-jobs! That's it! Now he's supposed to fork over 1.7 billion?! What about his family?! What about his children?! You don't think they have a right to that money?!

HERMES: Well, it's not like she'll ever actually see any money. I mean this thing has been working its way through the courts for years—right?

PLUTO: She's about to get it all. The whole thing. The Supreme Court just ruled in her favor. It's pretty much a done deal.

HERMES: Good for her.

PLUTO: Maybe not.

HERMES: What do you mean?

PLUTO: Well, I was thinking … what if I was to bring her down a little early—teach her a lesson?

HERMES: Are you serious?!

PLUTO: Why not?

HERMES: It seems a little unethical. Besides, won't anyone be suspicious? I mean, she's not even forty?

PLUTO: People die all the time.

HERMES: It just seems a shame to ruin that body of hers.

PLUTO: It's perfect justice for once! What business did she have interfering with this family's inheritance! What business did she have praying for the old man's death?! It would send a message to all the other gold diggers up there looking for easy prey!

HERMES: Well, I'm still not convinced the billionaire was the victim here, but I have to admit—I wouldn't mind having Anna Nicole around to look at. At least until the flesh starts rotting off.

PLUTO: It's decided, then.

HERMES: Say no more, Pluto—I'll fetch her for you.

PLUTO: I knew I could count on you.

* * *

VI

[ANNA NICOLE SMITH. PLUTO.]

ANNA NICOLE SMITH: Are you fucking kidding me?! This isn't fair! How is this fair?! I'm not even forty fucking years old!

PLUTO: Nothing could be more fair.

ANNA NICOLE SMITH: But I was about to inherit billions of dollars!

PLUTO: Exactly. Billions of dollars from your late husband's estate—the same husband whose death you used to pray for daily.

ANNA NICOLE SMITH: I did not!

PLUTO: Yes, you did.

ANNA NICOLE SMITH: How ... how do you know that?

PLUTO: I'm ruler of the underworld, sweetheart. I know everything.

ANNA NICOLE SMITH: Well ... so what if I did? I mean, he was almost dead anyway.

PLUTO: And now—so are you.

ANNA NICOLE SMITH: You think this is funny?!

PLUTO: A little bit.

ANNA NICOLE SMITH: I ought to climb up there and kick your ass!

PLUTO: Blow me.

ANNA NICOLE SMITH: You'd like that—wouldn't you!

PLUTO: Maybe. But I don't think my queen would appreciate it much.

ANNA NICOLE SMITH: Oh, you have a queen?

PLUTO: Of course. Persephone—you've heard of her?

ANNA NICOLE SMITH: No.

PLUTO: She's sort of famous. Have you heard of the seasons?

ANNA NICOLE SMITH: Is that a band?

PLUTO: No, the seasons—summer, winter, spring, fall?

ANNA NICOLE SMITH: Yeah?

PLUTO: She does that.

ANNA NICOLE SMITH: Is she hot?

PLUTO: She's … got that classical beauty.

ANNA NICOLE SMITH: So she's fat.

PLUTO: I didn't say that.

ANNA NICOLE SMITH: Classical beauty. That's what you said.

PLUTO: Yeah, but—

ANNA NICOLE SMITH: That means fat.

PLUTO: Okay, yes—she has a little weight problem. I've tried to keep her on the Weight Watchers, but she just gets so depressed—

ANNA NICOLE SMITH: All right, look—I'll make you a deal. Ditch the fat chick. Make me queen. I'll blow you all day long, you can do me in the ass—whatever. Just give me run of the palace, my own reality show, and tell that Hermes freak to smuggle some chocolate past that asshole ferryman of yours. The good shit. Perugina. Or Lindt.

PLUTO: Well … we did just get a new filmmaker down here.

ANNA NICOLE SMITH: Who?

PLUTO: Michael Moore.

ANNA NICOLE SMITH: No shit?! I love his stuff! I don't understand it—but he's so controversial!

PLUTO: I'll see what I can do.

* * *

VII

[LORD MARLBOROUGH. LORD DINWITTY.]

LORD MARLBOROUGH: Lord Dinwitty!

LORD DINWITTY: Lord Marlborough!

LORD MARLBOROUGH: Pleasure to see you, you drunken old sot! I had no idea you'd joined us down here!

LORD DINWITTY: I'm afraid so.

LORD MARLBOROUGH: How did it happen? I suppose you heard how I died?

LORD DINWITTY: Bad case of indigestion—wasn't it?

LORD MARLBOROUGH: That's right! Ate myself to death! Busted a gut—quite literally! Ha-ha! But what about you?

LORD DINWITTY: I'd rather not talk about it.

LORD MARLBOROUGH: Still a sore subject—is it? Something embarrassing? C'mon, Dinwitty—it can't be much worse than mine.

LORD DINWITTY: You remember Lord Carlsbad? Lonely old bugger. Lots of money. No children.

LORD MARLBOROUGH: Of course. Quite a character.

LORD DINWITTY: Well, I'd spoken kindly to him on occasion— even took him out to dinner once or twice. He was so grateful that one day, quite out of the blue, he promised to make me his sole heir. His sole heir! He's worth millions, you understand! I couldn't believe my luck. I hadn't asked for it—never thought of it, really— but from that day forward, in order to show my appreciation, you know, I began to spend practically every waking moment in his company. I'd drop by first thing in the morning. We'd play checkers. Shuffleboard. At first, it wasn't so bad—not terribly exciting, but I'd just think of the money, and that would keep me going. After a few weeks, though, I began to run out of steam. He liked to tell war stories—never actually *fought* in the war, mind you—spent most of the war typing in some office in Liverpool. Try to imagine, if you will, war stories that involve mostly *typing*—an occasional flirtation with the frumpy secretary or a heated debate over the proper use of the semicolon. It was interminable! I knew I couldn't keep it up much longer. Still, the inheritance! I couldn't stop thinking about it! I'd already spent most of it in my head! I began thinking up ways to hurry him along, if you know what I mean. Little things, at first. I convinced him to take up cricket—thought the exertion might be too much for his heart. But it only made him healthier! Suddenly he looked ten years younger! I took him boating—thought he might fall in and drown—I even went so far as to rock the boat a little. But the old bugger had impeccable balance, and, worse luck, he always wore a lifejacket. I began to get desperate. Finally, I decided to approach the butler. He was an unhappy little man—bitter that he had himself been overlooked for the inheritance. Together, we concocted a plan.

LORD MARLBOROUGH: A plan?

LORD DINWITTY: Are you familiar with ricin? No? It's a powerful poison—extracted from castor beans, of all things—twice as deadly as cobra venom! The butler agreed to administer the poison the next time his master called for wine—which he did constantly. He was a drunken sot. In return, I promised to reward the poor fellow for all his years of loyal service—something his master had never done.

LORD MARLBOROUGH: This is interesting—what happened next?

LORD DINWITTY: The next evening, after our usual activities, the servant brought two cups—the poisoned one for Carlsbad—and the other for me. Unfortunately, the incompetent oaf got nervous, switched the cups somehow—gave *me* the poisoned cup, and a few minutes later, much to my surprise, there I was—dead on the floor and cheated out of my inheritance.

[LORD MARLBOROUGH laughs.]

I suppose you think it's very funny. So did the old man. After he got over the initial shock, he put it all together, I guess, and laughed hysterically at his butler's mistake.

LORD MARLBOROUGH: Ah, my friend—short cuts are always dangerous. The high road would have been safer, if not quite so quick.

* * *

VIII

[JETHRO. BILLY-BOB.]

JETHRO: Tarnation! Fry mah hide!

BILLY-BOB: Jethro—whut's wrong?

JETHRO: Whut's wrong?! Whut's WRONG?! I'll tell yuh whut's wrong—ah dun been play'd th' fool! Fry mah hide! Ah lef' mah intire fortun' to a dadburn stranger—pickup an' all!

BILLY-BOB: How'd it happen?

JETHRO: Wal, ah been speculatin' on th' death o' thet big-shot actor fella what jest moved in over whar Bubba used ter live.

BILLY-BOB: Th' rich feller?

JETHRO: Yup. He nevah had no chilluns, so ah thunk ah had a decent shot—an' he seemed open t'mah ovahtures o' friendship. Ennyway, mah gal suggested ah make him th' benefishery o' mah will—yuh know, in th' hopes o' 'spirin' him t'do th' same fer me.

BILLY-BOB: Did it work?

JETHRO: Hell eff'n ah know! Mah roof caved in—killed me daid! Now thet city fucker gits ever'thin'! Th' pike done swallered hook an' bait!

BILLY-BOB: An' th' fisherman too, ah reckon! Wal, yuh knows whut they say …

JETHRO: Whut's thet?

BILLY-BOB: Th' pit yuh dig fo' t'other …

JETHRO: Fry mah hide!

IX

[MR. BEAN. MR. BASS.]

MR. BEAN: Mr. Bass! You finally decided to join us! You must be—what? Nearly a hundred!

MR. BASS: Ninety-eight.

MR. BEAN: Impressive! You beat me by almost thirty years!

MR. BASS: You missed out, Mr. Bean—the golden years were really something!

MR. BEAN: Personally, I was happy to go out in my prime. I don't know how you managed to find any joy in your last few years—old, weak, and childless.

MR. BASS: Oh, it wasn't as bad as all that. I could do what I liked—there were still plenty of beautiful women and fine bottles of wine to enjoy. I became known for my extravagant parties.

MR. BEAN: That *is* a change! In my day, you were known as a penny pincher.

MR. BASS: Oh, I never paid a penny out of my own pocket. All of these things were gifts, you see, from my many admirers.

MR. BEAN: You had admirers?

MR. BASS: Of course. Lots of them.

MR. BEAN: *You?* An old man with hardly a tooth left in his head?

MR. BASS: That's right.

MR. BEAN: They must have been frightful themselves.

MR. BASS: Oh, no—only the cream of the crop was allowed in my presence! The best society had to offer! The brightest and most beautiful! Young gods and goddesses—all eager to please! They had eyes only for me!

MR. BEAN: Did you invent some sort of fountain of youth?

MR. BASS: No, I was just as you see me now—old, bald, bleary-eyed, arthritic … and the object of all desire. I had to beat them off with a stick.

MR. BEAN: You're full of shit.

MR. BASS: Why, Mr. Bean—I should have thought you knew the violent passion for old men who have plenty of money and no children.

MR. BEAN: Ah! I see! Now I understand you! They were after your money!

MR. BASS: Of course—what else? But I assure you, Mr. Bean, I nevertheless took a great deal of satisfaction in my young lovers. They idolized me. Showered me with gifts. Threw parties. I had an almost godlike power over them. They couldn't refuse me anything—a discovery that came in particularly handy with the ladies. Sometimes I would play games—cut some of them off. Such rivalries! You wouldn't believe! Such jealous competition!

MR. BEAN: And how did you dispose of your fortune in the end?

MR. BASS: I promised to make each of them my sole heir—and they believed me! Every one of them! The little piggies! If they'd ever had an honest conversation with each other, they would have figured it out—but they didn't! They just pranced around, secretly laughing at the others—secure in the knowledge that they would win out in the end! Of course, my actual will told them all to go hang.

MR. BEAN: Who was the actual beneficiary? One of your relatives?

MR. BASS: No—my maid. Beautiful girl.

MR. BEAN: How old?

MR. BASS: About twenty.

MR. BEAN: Ah, I can guess her job description!

MR. BASS: Well, I'll say this—she deserved the money more than they did. She didn't love me either, of course—but she was honest about the whole thing. She didn't put on airs like the rest of them. And they all treated her like dirt. Now they can kiss her ass!

* * *

X

[CHARON. HERMES. MICHAEL MOORE.
Various Shades.]

CHARON: All right, listen up! All of you! This boat is small and leaky, and three-parts rotten—the slightest movement, and she'll capsize. So all this luggage you've brought stays put.

SADDAM HUSSEIN: What?!

SIGMUND FREUD: That isn't fair!

CHARON: Look, if you come on board with that stuff, believe me, you'll regret it—especially those of you who haven't learned to swim.

GENERAL PATTON: Then how are we supposed to cross?

CHARON: Leave all this junk behind—you won't need it anyway. Besides, there's no room to spare. Hermes, here, will clear you to board once you've stripped down to the bare essentials. And this fellow here—what's your name again?

MICHAEL MOORE: Michael Moore.

CHARON: He's making a documentary or something. Just ignore him.

HERMES: All right—who's first?

MARILYN MONROE: Me, I guess.

MICHAEL MOORE: Hey! Aren't you—

MARILYN MONROE: Marilyn Monroe—that's right.

HERMES: From Hollywood!

CHARON: Where's Hollywood?

MARILYN MONROE: Hollywood's a place where they'll pay you a thousand dollars for a kiss, and fifty cents for your soul.

CHARON: Here, you won't get a wooden nickel for either.

MARILYN MONROE: Can I board now?

HERMES: Sure—go ahead.

CHARON: Hermes!

HERMES: All right, fine!
                    [To MARILYN MONROE.]
I can't let you pass until you take that beauty off.

MARILYN MONROE: What?

CHARON: Take your beauty off!

HERMES: The lips, the kisses, the blond hair.

MARILYN MONROE: Take it off?

CHARON: Take it off!

HERMES: That's right. The mole, too. Now, the blushing cheeks. All the skin, actually. Good enough for you, Charon?

CHARON: She can pass.

HERMES: All right—next in line. Who's the gentleman in the royal get-up?

SADDAM HUSSEIN: I am Saddam Hussein, President of Iraq.

GENERAL PATTON: President! Tyrant's more like it!

SADDAM HUSSEIN: I may have been a tyrant, but I didn't do half the things your country accused me of!

CHARON: That's enough! Your political squabbles mean nothing down here!

SADDAM HUSSEIN: Fine.

GENERAL PATTON: Fine.

HERMES: What's all this splendor doing here, Saddam?

SADDAM HUSSEIN: Would you have a "tyrant" meet his end stripped bare?

HERMES: A tyrant? No, that would be asking too much. But with a shade, we must insist. Off with these trappings.

SADDAM HUSSEIN: If you insist. There goes my wealth.

HERMES: Pomp goes too, and pride; we'll capsize otherwise.

SADDAM HUSSEIN: At least let me keep my presidential insignia.

HERMES: No! Off it goes!

SADDAM HUSSEIN: Fine. That's everything—look for yourself.

HERMES: There's more yet: cruelty, oppression, violence.

SADDAM HUSSEIN: There then—I am bare.

HERMES: Pass on. And who might you be, my bulky friend?

JOHNNY UNITAS: Johnny Unitas—the football player.

HERMES: I know who you are! I saw the 1958 championship game! Against the Giants!

JOHNNY UNITAS: You were pulling for the Colts, I hope?

HERMES: You bet! Greatest game ever played!

JOHNNY UNITAS: Thanks. Well, I've stripped to nothing—mind if I pass?

CHARON: Stripped to nothing?! What about all that fleshy encumbrance?!

JOHNNY UNITAS: What do you mean?

CHARON: All those muscles and tendons! We'll sink to the bottom if you put one foot aboard! And those trophies and victories! Remove them!

JOHNNY UNITAS: There. No mistake about it now—I'm as light as any shade among you.

CHARON: That's more like it!

HERMES: On board with you, then. Now—what's this? Are you in full armor? And what's with all these guns and ammunition? You can't be serious?!

GENERAL PATTON: I'm a great general! A war hero! My country's pride!

HERMES: We're at peace in the underworld—no need for arms down here. The medals and accommodations have to go too. There—you can pass. Now, who is this? Some reverend sage?

MICHAEL MOORE: His name's Freud. He's a famous psychologist—and a quack. He thinks you want to pork your mother.

HERMES: Excuse me?!

SIGMUND FREUD: It's true—you do.

MICHAEL MOORE: Have him take off that cloak, and you'll find plenty to amuse yourself underneath.

HERMES: Well, sir—off with your clothes! Let's have a look!

MICHAEL MOORE: Do you think he's compensating for something?!

HERMES: My god! What a bundle! Quackery, ignorance, vanity, pride, idle probing, deceptive arguments, belligerence, humbug and and wishy-washy hair-splittings without end—and a bit of cocaine if I'm not mistaken! Why there's avarice, self-indulgence, impudence! Luxury! Peevishness! Yes, I see them all—no use trying to hide them, sir! Away with falsehood and swagger and snobbish intellectualism—why, you'd need an ocean liner to hold all this luggage!

SIGMUND FREUD: I relinquish them all, since that is your desire.

MICHAEL MOORE: Have his beard too, Hermes—there must be a good five pounds in that thing.

HERMES: Yes—the beard must go.

SIGMUND FREUD: And who will shave me?

HERMES: The General, here—he'll shoot it off. Someone toss him his gun.

MICHAEL MOORE: Oh! Can't I do it, Hermes? Please!

HERMES: No, the General must serve. Shrewdly shot! You look more like a man and less like a goat already.

MICHAEL MOORE: A little off the eyebrows?

HERMES: Why not? It'll save us another pound or two. Worm! Stop sniveling! What—are you afraid of death? Oh, get on board already!

MICHAEL MOORE: He still has the biggest thumper of all under his arm.

HERMES: What's that?

MICHAEL MOORE: Flattery! Many is the good turn it's done him.

SIGMUND FREUD: Oh, all right, Mr. Moore—suppose you leave your independence behind, and your plain-speaking, and your jests! No one else here has a jest about him!

HERMES: Don't listen to him, Michael! You keep your jests—useful commodities, those. All right—loose the cable and pull in the gangway! Haul up the anchor! Spread sail! Good luck on your voyage! What are you all whining about? You fools! You, the psychologist, late of the beard—you're as bad as any of them!

SIGMUND FREUD: Ah, Hermes—I had secretly hoped that the soul was immortal.

MICHAEL MOORE: Liar! That's not what's upsetting him.

HERMES: No? What then?

MICHAEL MOORE: He knows he'll never have a good dinner again—never sneak out at night, with his cloak over his head, to make the rounds of the brothels—he'll never cheat good people out of their hard-earned money again, pretending to interpret their dreams—

SIGMUND FREUD: And tell me, Mr. Moore, are *you* content to be dead?

MICHAEL MOORE: I guess so, since I came here on purpose.

SIGMUND FREUD: What was that sound?

MICHAEL MOORE: Was that a crowd shouting somewhere on earth?

HERMES: It was. The tyrant's funeral. His death was somewhat controversial, it seems. Some are applauding his execution—others believe him a martyr and are swearing revenge. So it goes.

CHARON: Let's go! We're wasting time! There'll be another load coming soon!

* * *

XI

[CRATES. DIOGENES.]

CRATES: Diogenes … did you know Moerichus of Corinth?

DIOGENES: Who?

CRATES: A ship-owner, rolling in money. He had a cousin named Aristeas, nearly as rich.

DIOGENES: I don't recall.

CRATES: They were about the same age, and each expected to inherit the other's wealth if he should die. They published their wills simultaneously, each naming the other as sole heir. They took great pride in showing public respect to one another—it became a sort of spectacle, each trying to outdo the other cousin in his show of affection.

DIOGENES: That's right. Public opinion went back and forth—first Aristeas would take the lead, then Moerichus would pull ahead. How did it end? I don't remember.

CRATES: They both died the same day—a storm came up suddenly and capsized them mid-channel—the properties passed to two other cousins, distant relations with no knowledge of the whole affair.

DIOGENES: That's the way it goes—isn't it?

CRATES: I don't understand this obsession with inheritance.

DIOGENES: Especially since it usually requires a loved one to die.

CRATES: When we were alive, we never had such designs on one another.

DIOGENES: No, I never prayed for Antisthenes' death with a view to inheriting his staff—although it was a very nice one he'd cut himself from a wild olive—and I don't think you ever had had an eye to my succession, even though it included a tub and two pints of beans.

CRATES: No, but the important things you inherited from Antisthenes, and I from you—and in those treasures was more grandeur and majesty than in the Persian Empire.

DIOGENES: You mean—

CRATES: Wisdom, independence, truth, frankness, freedom of thought.

DIOGENES: I did inherit all that from Antisthenes. And left it to you with some addition, I hope.

CRATES: But no one recognized these treasures. We weren't lavished with gifts from expectant heirs—they all had their eyes on gold instead.

DIOGENES: They had no receptacle for such gifts as we could offer. Luxury had made them leaky—as full of holes as a worn-out bucket! Put wisdom, frankness, or truth into them, and it would have dropped right out the bottom!

CRATES: But gold they could grip somehow.

DIOGENES: Or so they thought.

CRATES: Yes—our wealth will still be ours down here, while they arrive with no more than a penny—and that for the ferryman.

* * *

XII

[ALEXANDER. HANNIBAL. MINOS. SCIPIO.]

ALEXANDER: Stand aside, Libyan.

HANNIBAL: You stand aside.

ALEXANDER: I claim precedence.

HANNIBAL: Precedence?

ALEXANDER: That's right.

HANNIBAL: On what grounds?

ALEXANDER: On the grounds that I'm the better man.

HANNIBAL: Hah!

ALEXANDER: You disagree?

HANNIBAL: It's not even close.

ALEXANDER: Fine—let Minos decide.

MINOS: Me? I don't even know who the two of you are.

ALEXANDER: This is Hannibal, the Carthaginian. And I'm Alexander, son of Philip.

MINOS: Alexander the Great?

ALEXANDER: That's right.

HANNIBAL: Pfff!

MINOS: Wow! What a pair! What's the quarrel about?

ALEXANDER: It's a question of precedence. He claims to be the superior general. I maintain that I am without equal.

MINOS: Well, you'll each have your say. The Lesbian first.

HANNIBAL: Libyan.

MINOS: Go ahead.

HANNIBAL: All right. I think we can all agree that the highest praise is due to those who have fought their way to greatness from obscurity—who have pulled themselves up by their own bootstraps—clothed themselves in power, and proven themselves worthy of that authority. I entered Spain with only a handful of men, fought bravely, proved myself a leader, and eventually—as a result of my exploits—was honored with the supreme command. I conquered the Celtiberians, subdued Western Gaul, crossed the Alps, overran the valley of the Po, sacked town after town, made myself master of the plains, approached the bulwarks of the capital, and in one day slew such a host that their finger-rings were measured by bushels, and the rivers were bridged by their bodies. Unlike Alexander here, I never pretended to be a god, never related visions of my mother—I made no secret of the fact that I was mere flesh and blood. My rivals were the most capable generals in the world, commanding the best soldiers in the world. I never warred with Medes or Assyrians, who fly before they are pursued and yield the victory to anyone with the courage to take it. Alexander, on the other hand, in increasing and extending the dominion he inherited from his father, was merely following the path set out for him by Fortune. This "fabled conqueror" no sooner crushed his puny adversaries in the victories of Issus and Arbela, than he forsook the traditions of his country and lived the life of a Persian, accepting the worship of his subjects, handing his friends over to the executioner, or even assassinating them at his own table! I always respected the freedom of my country—never attempted to subjugate her for my own personal glory. I answered when she called. And when the enemy with their huge armament invaded Libya, I laid aside the privileges of my office and submitted to my sentence without a murmur. Yet Alexander would call me a barbarian because I'm unskilled in Greek culture—because I couldn't recite Homer. I admit,

I never enjoyed the advantages of Aristotle's instruction like he did. I had to make due with such qualities as were mine by nature. And it is on these grounds that I claim pre-eminence. I do not deny that my rival has all the luster that attaches to the wearing of a diadem, and I've been told that, for Macedonians, such things have charms. But I refuse to believe this constitutes a higher claim than the courage and genius of one who owed nothing to Fortune, and everything to his own resolution.

MINOS: Not bad, for a Lesbian.

HANNIBAL: Libyan.

MINOS: Right. Alexander—what do you say to that?

ALEXANDER: Silence, Minos, would be the best answer to such a boastful tongue. All the world knows of my Fame—that alone should suffice to prove I was a great prince, and my opponent a petty adventurer. But I would have you consider the gulf between us. I was only a boy when called to the throne—and yet I successfully quelled the disorders of my kingdom and avenged my father's murder. By the destruction of Thebes, I inspired such awe among the Greeks that they appointed me their commander-in-chief. From that moment forward, scorning to confine myself to the kingdom I had inherited from my father, I extended my gaze over the entire face of the earth! Nothing but the whole of it would quench my ambition! I dared to invade Asia and, with only a modest force, gained a great victory on the Granicus, took Lydia, Ionia, Phrygia—in short, subdued all that was within my reach. I marched for Issus, where Darius waited at the head of his myriads. You know the result of that confrontation—any historian can tell you the number of dead I dispatched on that bloody day. The ferryman says his boat wouldn't hold them—most had to cross to the underworld on rafts of their own construction. I was ever at the head of my troops, ever courted danger. I penetrated into India, and carried my empire to the shores of Ocean. I captured elephants. I conquered Porus. I crossed the Tanais, and worsted the Scythians— no mean enemies. I heaped benefits on my friends, but wasn't afraid to punish my enemies. If men mistook me for a god, well—who can blame them? The grandeur of my victories might excuse such a belief. But to conclude, I died a king—Hannibal, a fugitive—fitting end for such a villain. Of his Italian victories I will say only this— they were not the fruit of honest warfare, but of treachery, craft, and deceit. He accuses me of self-indulgence, but it's well known that he and his soldiers grew soft and fat wooing the ladies of Capua while the Romans gathered their army. Had I not scorned the Western world and turned my attention to the East, I could easily have conquered his Italy, Libya, and everything else as far West as Gades—but nations that already cowered beneath a master were unworthy of my sword. That's all. I will say nothing more. Of the many arguments I might have used, these shall suffice. Minos, I await your decision.

SCIPIO: Minos, can I say a few words before you issue your judgment?

MINOS: Who are you?

SCIPIO: Scipio, the Roman general who destroyed Carthage and gained great victories over the Libyans.

MINOS: Well—what do you have to say?

SCIPIO: Just this—that Alexander is my superior, and I am Hannibal's, having defeated him, and forced him to flee like the coward he is.

HANNIBAL: It was a strategic retreat!

SCIPIO: What impudence! To contend with Alexander, to whom I, your conqueror, would not presume to compare myself!

MINOS: Well spoken, Scipio! All right, then—I guess that clears it up. Alexander comes first, you next; and I think we'll put Hannibal third.

* * *

XIII

[DIOGENES. ALEXANDER.]

DIOGENES: Alexander! Is it really true? *You're* dead like the rest of us?

ALEXANDER: Is there anything unusual about a mortal dying?

DIOGENES: So Ammon lied when he said you were his son? You were Philip's after all?

ALEXANDER: Apparently so. If I had been Ammon's, I wouldn't have died.

DIOGENES: But all those stories! The serpent visiting your mother in bed, impregnating her—all that! It seemed so plausible!

ALEXANDER: I've heard the stories. It was all moonshine.

DIOGENES: Well, at least it served some practical purpose. Your divinity brought a good many people to their knees.

ALEXANDER: It did make things easier.

DIOGENES: I'm just curious—who did you leave your empire to?

ALEXANDER: I wish I knew. I didn't have time to leave behind any instructions.

DIOGENES: You died suddenly then?

ALEXANDER: Suspiciously so. I suspect I was poisoned, but I can't be sure. It could have been something I picked up from one of those Babylonian whores. Anyway, I barely had time to pass my ring to Perdiccas before I dropped dead. Why are you laughing?

DIOGENES: Oh, nothing—I'm sorry. I was just thinking how my fellow Greeks flattered you and threw themselves at your feet! What a bunch of asses! They were so sure you were a god! One of the twelve, they insisted! The Serpent's son!

ALEXANDER: I'm glad you're amused.

DIOGENES: Do you mind if I ask where you're buried?

ALEXANDER: Babylon. But Ptolemy of the Guards has sworn to have my remains removed to Egypt—a more appropriate resting place for one reckoned among the Gods.

DIOGENES: Still nursing some hope of developing into an Osiris or an Anubis?

ALEXANDER: Don't mock me.

DIOGENES: Give it up, your Godhead! Once you've crossed the Styx and penetrated the gates of Hades, that's it—there's no leaving! Cerberus makes sure of that. Besides, Ptolemy has long since passed away himself.

ALEXANDER: What—already?!

DIOGENES: *Already?* You do realize you've been dead for several thousand years now—don't you?

ALEXANDER: Has it been that long? Really? It seems like only yesterday I was leading my troops into battle.

DIOGENES: Time passes quickly here.

ALEXANDER: I'll say.

DIOGENES: I'm curious—what do you miss most about that earthly bliss you left behind? The glorious battles? The guards and armor-bearers? The heaps of gold and adoring subjects? The elephants? The purple cloaks? The whores?

ALEXANDER: I'd like to say the battles. But probably the whores.

DIOGENES: Does the thought of them hurt?

ALEXANDER: What I wouldn't give for one more night with a woman—any woman!

DIOGENES: What—are you crying?

ALEXANDER: No—I have something in my eye.

DIOGENES: Of course. Listen, I'll tell you a little secret—the waters of our rivers down here have certain hallucinogenic properties. Take a few good, deep, repeated draughts of Lethe-water and you may find yourself with your harem once more!

ALEXANDER: Oh, no—here they come again!

DIOGENES: Who?

ALEXANDER: That mob of soldiers! They keep chasing me and trying to tear off my limbs! I'd like to know what I ever did to them!

DIOGENES: You killed them.

ALEXANDER: What?

DIOGENES: Those are all the soldiers you killed on the battlefield. They want revenge.

ALEXANDER: Oh. Well ... I should probably be going then.

DIOGENES: All right. But remember—repeated draughts.

* * *

XIV

[PHILIP. ALEXANDER.]

PHILIP: Well, son ... do you mind if I call you "son" now?

ALEXANDER: Knock yourself out.

PHILIP: You finally admit it then?

ALEXANDER: Why not?

PHILIP: If you were Ammon's, you couldn't have died—you wouldn't be here.

ALEXANDER: Look, I knew all along you were my father. I only accepted the word of the oracle because I thought it was good policy.

PHILIP: Good policy? To be fooled by lying priests?

ALEXANDER: You have to admit—it had an awe-inspiring effect on the barbarians. When they thought they had a God to deal with, they gave up without much of a fight. It made the whole conquest thing a lot easier.

PHILIP: It might not have been so effective if your adversaries had been a little more worthy.

ALEXANDER: What's that supposed to mean?

PHILIP: Who did you ever conquer that was worth conquering?

ALEXANDER: Oh, please.

PHILIP: You fought weak-minded barbarians—timid things with puny bows and wicker shields. Believe me, it was something altogether different conquering the Greeks: Boeotians, Phocians, Athenians, Arcadian hoplites, Thessalian cavalry, javelin-men from

Elis, peltasts of Mantinea, Thracians, Illyrians, Paeonians. To subdue *those* foes was something to be proud of!

ALEXANDER: What about the Scythians? Or the Indian elephants—they were no joke! And *my* conquests weren't gained by treachery or deceit! I never broke an oath or purchased victory at the expense of honor. As for the Greeks, I'm sure you've heard how I handled Thebes?

PHILIP: Yes, I heard all about it from Clitus.

ALEXANDER: Who?

PHILIP: Clitus.

ALEXANDER: Name doesn't ring a bell.

PHILIP: You skewered him in the middle of dinner—

ALEXANDER: Oh. *Him.*

PHILIP: —because he dared to mention my achievements in the same breath as yours.

ALEXANDER: What do you want me to say? I was in a mood.

PHILIP: They also tell me you took to aping the manners of your conquered Medes, abandoned your Macedonian cloak in favor of the *candies*, assumed the upright tiara, and exacted oriental prostrations from Macedonian freemen! Some king! As for your whores, your beloved Hephaestion, and your scholars in lions' cages—the less said the better. I have to admit, there were times I hoped you really were Ammon's son—and not mine.

ALEXANDER: What about my bravery in battle? That had to make you proud! Did you know I was the first to leap down the ramparts of Oxydracae? I was covered with wounds—nearly died!

PHILIP: That was a bad move, if you ask me.

ALEXANDER: I guess I can't do anything right!

PHILIP: You were passing yourself off as a God. Being wounded and carried off the field, bleeding and groaning, could only excite the ridicule of anyone unfortunate enough to witness the spectacle. The son of Zeus in a swoon—requiring medical assistance! Who could help but laugh at that? And now that you've died, well, you can guess all the jokes being cracked about your divinity!

ALEXANDER: That will pass. History will rank me with Heracles and Dionysus—even higher! I took Aornos, which was more than either of them could do!

PHILIP: Spoken like the true son of Ammon! Heracles and Dionysus! Pfff! Still putting on airs—aren't you?! Even now when you're nothing but a corpse!

* * *

XV

[A gathering of playwrights.]

WILLIAM SHAKESPEARE: Death is a fearful thing.

JOHN DRYDEN: Death, in itself, is nothing; but we fear,
To be we know not what, we know not where.

EUGENE IONESCO: There are more dead people than living. And their numbers are increasing. The living are getting rarer.

LEONID ANDREYEV: Death augments distance and dulls the memory. Death reconciles.

PIERRE CORNEILLE: Each instant of life is a step toward death.

EURIPIDES: Who knows but life be that which men call death,
And death what men call life?

TENNESSEE WILLIAMS: The human animal is a beast that dies but the fact that he's dying don't give him pity for others, no sir.

WILLIAM SHAKESPEARE: Cowards die many times before their deaths—the valiant never taste of death but once.

JEAN COCTEAU: Everything one does in life, even love, occurs in an express train racing toward death.

PLAUTUS: Life itself is held in the grinning fangs of Death.

LUIGI PIRANDELLO: As soon as one is born, one starts dying!

EUGENE IONESCO: No society has been able to abolish human sadness, no political system can deliver us from the pain of living, from our fear of death, our thirst for the absolute. It is the human condition that directs the social condition, not vice versa.

IVAN TURGENEV: Go and try to disprove death. Death will disprove you.

AUGUST WILSON: Death ain't nothing but a fastball on the outside corner.

JOHN WEBSTER: I know death has ten thousand several doors for men to take their exits.

WILLIAM SHAKESPEARE: The stroke of death is as a lover's pinch, which hurts and is desired.

SOPHOCLES: Not even old age knows how to love death.

AESCHYLUS: Death is easier than a wretched life—better never to have born than to live and fare badly.

EUGENE IONESCO: Since the death instinct exists in the heart of everything that lives, since we suffer from trying to repress it, since everything that lives longs for rest, let us unfasten the ties that bind us to life, let us cultivate our death wish, let us develop it, water it like a plant, let it grow unhindered. Suffering and fear are born from the repression of the death wish.

PLAUTUS: He whom the gods favor dies in youth.

J.M. BARRIE: To die is an awfully big adventure.

VICTOR HUGO: Our life dreams the Utopia. Our death achieves the Ideal.

WILLIAM SHAKESPEARE: How oft when they were at the point of death, have men been merry!

GEORGE BERNARD SHAW: Life does not cease to be funny when people die any more than it ceases to be serious when people laugh.

JOHN DRYDEN: The world's an inn, and death the journey's end.

EDWARD ALBEE: That's the happiest moment. When it's all done. When we stop. When we can stop.

* * *

XVI

[MICHAEL MOORE. HERCULES.]

MICHAEL MOORE: Hey! I'd recognize that club and lion's skin anywhere! You must be Hercules?!

HERCULES: That's right.

MICHAEL MOORE: Wow! You're gigantic!

HERCULES: You should have seen me during my twelve labours—I was really buff then! I need to start hitting the weights, but it's hard to motivate myself down here. Plus, I have to compete with all these athletes down here on Human Growth Hormone—they're such cheaters!

MICHAEL MOORE: What are you doing down here anyway?

HERCULES: What do you mean?

MICHAEL MOORE: Well, I must be a little confused about my mythology—I thought you were a God.

HERCULES: Half-god. Zeus was my father, but my mother was mortal. Alcmena—daughter of Electryon, king of Mycenae and a son of Perseus.

MICHAEL MOORE: But … if you're a God—

HERCULES: Half-god.

MICHAEL MOORE: Half-god. Shouldn't you be—

HERCULES: In Heaven?

MICHAEL MOORE: Yeah.

HERCULES: I am. Sort of. Hercules is with the Gods in Heaven. And he's got a hot little piece of ass for a wife—white-ankled Hebe! Have you heard of her?

MICHAEL MOORE: No, I—

HERCULES: She's really something—never ages! She's always eighteen, and get this—she's an eternal virgin—you pop her cherry and it grows right back!

MICHAEL MOORE: That *is* something.

HERCULES: That's what I'm saying.

MICHAEL MOORE: But if Hercules is in Heaven—

HERCULES: I'm his phantom.

MICHAEL MOORE: His phantom!

HERCULES: His shadowy mortal half.

MICHAEL MOORE: I don't understand. There are two of you?

HERCULES: Two halves. The eternal half still lives. The mortal half, you see before you.

MICHAEL MOORE: Well, you sure got the short end of the stick!

HERCULES: What do you mean?

MICHAEL MOORE: Well, your other half's up in Heaven popping cherries—while you're down here rotting away.

HERCULES: I never thought of it like that. It does seem unfair—doesn't it?

MICHAEL MOORE: I'll say.

HERCULES: But what am I supposed to do about it?

MICHAEL MOORE: I don't know. Maybe you could work out some kind of time-share thing.

HERCULES: Hey—that's not a bad idea! I'll go talk to him about it right now!

MICHAEL MOORE: Good for you. And listen, if he refuses and you need any help raising a stink about the whole thing, just let me know—that's what I do.

* * *

XVII

[MICHAEL MOORE. TANTALUS.]

MICHAEL MOORE: Tantalus! What's with all the wailing and gnashing of teeth? I'm trying to get a little shuteye!

TANTALUS: Ah! I'm so thirsty!

MICHAEL MOORE: Have you considered maybe bending down and taking a drink from that pool of water at your feet?

TANTALUS: Do you think I'm stupid?! The water shrinks away as soon as it sees me coming! And if I do manage to scoop some up, it evaporates in my hands before I can get it into my mouth!

MICHAEL MOORE: Well, what do you care anyway? You're a shade. You have no body—you don't need nourishment. The part of you that was susceptible to hunger and thirst has long since been eaten by worms!

TANTALUS: That's my punishment! Don't you see—the soul thirsts as if it were the body!

MICHAEL MOORE: Oh. That sucks, man.

TANTALUS: What I wouldn't give for one drop of water!

MICHAEL MOORE: Still, it's not like anything can *happen* to you. I mean, it's not like you can *die* of thirst. I don't know of any second Hades—you can't die in this one and move on to another.

TANTALUS: That's a very logical argument. But you can't reason with me. It's all part of the sentence—I must long for a drink even though I don't need it.

MICHAEL MOORE: But if you understand the fallacy of your desire, why can't you learn to control it?

TANTALUS: You ask too much of me.

MICHAEL MOORE: I suppose you're right. It's not that unusual, after all—we all want what we can't have.

* * *

XVIII

[MICHAEL MOORE. HERMES.]

MICHAEL MOORE: Hermes! Hey! I've been looking all over for you! I was wondering if you could do me a little favor! I've been here for a while now, and I still haven't seen any of the great beauties of history.

HERMES: I'm a little busy right now.

MICHAEL MOORE: Can't you just point out a few of the famous ladies? For my documentary—you know. It might get you some screen time.

HERMES: Fine—look over there.

MICHAEL MOORE: Where?

HERMES: There—Nefertiti, Cleopatra, Helen, Leda—all the beauties of old. Birds of a feather, you know.

MICHAEL MOORE: I don't see anything—just bones, and bare skulls.

HERMES: Those bones, as you call them, have inspired some of the greatest poetry the world has ever known.

MICHAEL MOORE: But they all look exactly alike!

HERMES: *Now* they do.

MICHAEL: But which one is Helen?

HERMES: That skull there.

MICHAEL MOORE: *That's* Helen of Troy? For *that*, a thousand ships carried warriors from every part of Greece? Greeks and barbarians were slain! Cities made desolate!

HERMES: Ah, Michael, you never saw the living Helen! If you had, you wouldn't say such things! She was a real marvel—the kind of beauty that comes along once a millennium! One smile from her, and you could die happy!

MICHAEL MOORE: I guess I'll have to take your word for it.

HERMES: We look at withered flowers. Their dye is gone. They're not much to look at now—ugly even. But in the hour of their bloom, these bare skulls were things of such beauty they gave men reason to live.

MICHAEL MOORE: Strange—isn't it?

HERMES: What's that?

MICHAEL MOORE: How quickly it all fades. Would the Greeks have gone to such lengths if they'd known Helen would come to this?

HERMES: I don't have time for moralizing. Choose a spot to lie down.

MICHAEL MOORE: I think I'll look around a little more first.

HERMES: Whatever—I have to fetch new dead.

* * *

XIX

[PROTESILAUS. MENELAUS. PARIS.
CLARENCE DARROW.]

CLARENCE DARROW: Now wait just a minute, young man—what do you mean assaulting Helen like that?

PROTESILAUS: I ought to kill that bitch!

CLARENCE DARROW: Judging from her appearance, I'd say she's already dead.

PROTESILAUS: I'll kill her again! I'll scatter her bones so she can't ever put herself back together! Haven't you ever been so angry you wanted to strangle someone?!

CLARENCE DARROW: I've never killed a man, but I have read many obituaries with great pleasure.

PROTESILAUS: Who are you anyway?

CLARENCE DARROW: Clarence Darrow—attorney at law.

PROTESILAUS: Who?

CLARENCE DARROW: Ever hear of the Scopes trial?

PROTESILAUS: No.

CLARENCE DARROW: Leopold and Loeb?

PROTESILAUS: No.

CLARENCE DARROW: The American Civil Liberties Union?

PROTESILAUS: *No.*

CLARENCE DARROW: You should get out more.

PROTESILAUS: You should mind your own business! What do you care if I throttle Helen?! It's none of your business!

CLARENCE DARROW: As long as the world shall last there will be wrongs, and if no man objected, those wrongs would last forever.

PROTESILAUS: Throttling her wouldn't be wrong—it would be justice! It's her fault I died, leaving my house half built and my bride a widow!

CLARENCE DARROW: Now hold on—let's reason this out. I'm a bit fuzzy on my ancient history, but wasn't Menelaus the one who dragged you all to war after his missing bride?

PROTESILAUS: I'll throttle him too!

MENELAUS: Don't be ridiculous! Paris is the one you want. He threw all law and morality to the wind when he seduced his host's wife and carried her off. If anyone deserves a throttling, it's *him*. And not just from you—he's responsible for so many deaths!

PROTESILAUS: You're right! It's Paris I want!

PARIS: Oh, come, sir—am I really to blame for falling in love. You know how vain it is to strive against the passions of the heart. Love draws us where it will.

MENELAUS: There's some truth to that.

PROTESILAUS: Dammit—if only I had Love himself here in these hands! I'd throttle him!

CLARENCE DARROW: Permit me to charge myself with his defense. He does not absolutely deny his responsibility for Paris' infatuation—but as for your death, Protesilaus, he refers you to yourself.

PROTESILAUS: How is it *my* fault?!

CLARENCE DARROW: You forgot all about your bride, left her all alone, sacrificed love for fame, and the moment the fleet touched the Troad, took that rash senseless leap which brought you first to shore and next to death.

PROTESILAUS: No, no, you've got it all wrong, Darrow. The blame doesn't rest with me, but with Fate—my thread was spun from the beginning.

CLARENCE DARROW: Exactly—so why blame our good friends here?

* * *

XX

[MICHAEL MOORE. CLARENCE DARROW.
Various Shades.]

MICHAEL MOORE: So, Clarence, you've been down here a while—
show me all the sights of Hades.

CLARENCE DARROW: That would be quite an undertaking. The
principal things you've seen already. You can't miss Cerberus, the
three-headed dog, or Charon, the ferryman who brought you over, and
you saw the River Styx on your way in.

MICHAEL MOORE: Yes, and I've seen the aristocrats, and the
tormented, and some of the great beauties. But what about the old
heroes?

CLARENCE DARROW: This is Agamemnon. This is Achilles.
Next to him is Ajax. And that pile you're standing on there—that's
Odysseus.

MICHAEL MOORE: Poor Homer! All his great heroes flung down
upon the earth, shapeless, undistinguishable—mere meaningless dust!
Who's this pile here?

CLARENCE DARROW: That's Xerxes.

MICHAEL MOORE: Ha! To think—these few fragile bones made
all of Greece tremble? I ought to give him a box on the ear!

CLARENCE DARROW: Don't! Poor thing! You'll crack his skull!

MICHAEL MOORE: What about the philosophers—are they around?

CLARENCE DARROW: Sure—there's Empedocles. He's half-
roasted.

MICHAEL MOORE: Looks like a peanut.

CLARENCE DARROW: He threw himself into an active volcano—Mount Etna.

MICHAEL MOORE: Tell me, friend—what made you jump?

EMPEDOCLES: I was depressed.

CLARENCE DARROW: Don't listen to him. He wanted people to think his body had vanished—that he'd turned into an immortal god—but the volcano threw back one of his bronze sandals, revealing the deceit.

MICHAEL MOORE: Bad luck.

EMPEDOCLES: I should have gone barefoot.

MICHAEL MOORE: What about Socrates—where's he?

CLARENCE DARROW: Usually bullshitting with Nestor and Palamedes.

MICHAEL MOORE: Could I see him?

CLARENCE DARROW: He's right there—the bald one?

MICHAEL MOORE: They're all bald!

CLARENCE DARROW: With the snub-nose.

SOCRATES: Are you looking for me?

MICHAEL MOORE: Socrates?

SOCRATES: That's right.

MICHAEL MOORE: Wow! It's a real honor!

SOCRATES: How are things on earth? Do they still talk about *me* every now and then?

MICHAEL MOORE: Sure—your teachings are the foundation of Western philosophy!

SOCRATES: Too bad—I told them I didn't know anything, but they wouldn't believe me. They thought I was being ironic.

MICHAEL MOORE: Who are your friends here?

SOCRATES: This is Plato.

PLATO: Hi.

SOCRATES: And that's Aristotle.

ARISTOTLE: What's up?

SOCRATES: Would you like to join us?

MICHAEL MOORE: No, thank you, but I think I'm going to take up a spot next to Midas, Howard Hughes and John D. Rockefeller—their wailing never ceases to amuse me.

CLARENCE DARROW: Well, I have to be off—I'll show you the rest some other day.

MICHAEL MOORE: I didn't mean to hold you up. I've seen enough.

* * *

XXI

[MICHAEL MOORE. CERBERUS.]

MICHAEL MOORE: Easy, boy—I just want to ask a few questions. I'm sure a God like you can do more than bark if he wants to.

CERBERUS: Sure—I can talk. What do you want to know?

MICHAEL MOORE: Tell me—how did Socrates behave during his descent?

CERBERUS: Are you sure you want to know? You may be disillusioned.

MICHAEL MOORE: I can take it.

CERBERUS: All right. Well, while he was some way off, he talked a good game—put on quite a show—kept spouting philosophy—said things like "To fear death, my friends, is only to think ourselves wise, without being wise: for it is to think that we know what we do not know." Then he passed through the gates and saw the gloom. I gave him a little push—he was poking along—and he started crying like a baby—whimpering and shaking all over! It was pretty pathetic.

MICHAEL MOORE: So it was all theory—when it came to the real thing, his indifference was a sham.

CERBERUS: That's right. Later, he accepted the inevitable and put a bold face on it—pretended to welcome the universal fate. But his entrance was pretty pathetic—and that's where the real test comes.

MICHAEL MOORE: What did you think of my performance?

CERBERUS: Ah, you were the exception, Michael! You're a credit to the breed—and so was Diogenes before you. The two of you came of your own free will, with a laugh for yourselves and a curse for the rest—that's the way to do it!

XXII

[CHARON. MICHAEL MOORE. HERMES.]

CHARON: Pay up, you rascal!

MICHAEL MOORE: Shout all you want—it won't do any good.

CHARON: I brought you across! Give me my fare!

MICHAEL MOORE: You should have collected beforehand. I haven't got it.

CHARON: Who's so poor that he hasn't got a penny?

MICHAEL MOORE: Me.

CHARON: Pay … or … or … by Pluto, I'll strangle you!

MICHAEL MOORE: I should probably mention that this camera is still rolling—now do you want to repeat that threat?

CHARON: I want my money!

MICHAEL MOORE: Let Hermes pay—he put me on board.

CHARON: *[To HERMES.]* Well?

HERMES: I'm not your fare collector!

CHARON: Fine, then—I won't let you off.

MICHAEL MOORE: Great. I'd love to ride around for a while—haven't got anything better to do.

CHARON: I'll put you to work! I'll give you an oar!

MICHAEL MOORE: Fine. I could use the exercise. But I still can't pay you—if I haven't got it, I haven't got it.

CHARON: You knew the price when you came onboard!

MICHAEL MOORE: Sure, I knew. But I had to cross. What was I supposed to do—not die?

CHARON: Do you really expect to be the only passenger ever to cross for free?

MICHAEL MOORE: What if I make you an associate producer on my documentary?

CHARON: I don't care about your stupid documentary! I want my penny!

MICHAEL MOORE: Well, I guess you'd better bring me back to life then.

CHARON: Oh, right—I'm sure Pluto will go for that! That's a great idea!

MICHAEL MOORE: Well, stop crying then.

CHARON: Where did you find this joker, Hermes? Did you hear the noise he made on the crossing—laughing and jeering at all the others, singing while they were bawling their eyes out!

HERMES: Ah, Charon, you little know your passenger! Independence, every inch of him!

CHARON: Wait till I catch you—

MICHAEL MOORE: Precisely. I'll wait—till you catch me again.

* * *

XXIII

[PLUTO. ANNA NICOLE SMITH. A FALLEN SOLDIER.]

PLUTO: Who are you and what do you want?

FALLEN SOLDIER: I'm a fallen soldier, sir. I was the first American to die in the Iraq War. Or the Second Gulf War. Whatever you want to call it.

ANNA NICOLE SMITH: The very first?

FALLEN SOLDIER: The very first, but only by a few seconds—three buddies died with me. Our chopper went down in Kuwait, two days after the war started.

PLUTO: Enemy fire?

FALLEN SOLDIER: No, sir. It was just bad luck, really—there was a lot of blowing sand and smoke from burning oil wells. We weren't used to it, got disoriented—then there was some kind of mechanical problem, and we went down.

ANNA NICOLE SMITH: That sucks!

FALLEN SOLDIER: Yes, ma'am.

ANNA NICOLE SMITH: You poor thing! You want a chocolate?

FALLEN SOLDIER: What?

ANNA NICOLE SMITH: A chocolate—it might make you feel better.

FALLEN SOLDIER: No … thank you.

PLUTO: What *do* you want from us?

FALLEN SOLDIER: Release and one day's life.

PLUTO: That's what everyone down here wants. It's not possible.

FALLEN SOLDIER: I ... I just want to see my family one more time—my wife and kids.

PLUTO: Just wait a little while, and they'll join you here. It's so simple—no need for you to go back up.

FALLEN SOLDIER: You don't understand ... I need to explain to my kids ... why it was necessary ... why I had to die ... they don't understand.

PLUTO: Why *did* you have to die?

FALLEN SOLDIER: I was protecting my country.

PLUTO: From who?

FALLEN SOLDIER: The Iraqis.

PLUTO: They're not very dangerous—are they?

FALLEN SOLDIER: Yes, sir—they had WMDs.

ANNA NICOLE SMITH: Huh? What's that? WM who?

FALLEN SOLDIER: Weapons of mass destruction.

ANNA NICOLE SMITH: Yikes! Are you sure you don't want a chocolate? They're *goooood.*

FALLEN SOLDIER: No, I—

PLUTO: There were no weapons of mass destruction.

FALLEN SOLDIER: What?

PLUTO: Don't take my word for it—read the Iraq Survey Group Report. There were no WMDs. They didn't have any.

FALLEN SOLDIER: What about their nuclear program?

PLUTO: Disbanded for years.

FALLEN SOLDIER: But ... President Bush said they bought uranium from Niger. We had intelligence.

PLUTO: Yeah. Turns out that wasn't true.

FALLEN SOLDIER: They had mobile labs—for germ warfare.

PLUTO: They had mobile labs—to produce hydrogen for artillery balloons.

FALLEN SOLDIER: Well ... still, they ... they had ties to Al Qaeda! They sponsored the 9-11 attacks!

PLUTO: Not so much.

FALLEN SOLDIER: No?

PLUTO: No.

FALLEN SOLDIER: Are you sure?

PLUTO: Your leaders mislead you, son. I'm sorry.
                    [Silence.]

FALLEN SOLDIER: I ... I just wanted to protect my country ... protect my wife and kids.
                    [Pause.]
I miss them so much.

PLUTO: Go back to your resting place. Be patient. They'll join you soon.

ANNA NICOLE SMITH: C'mon, Pluto—don't be such a hard-ass. Can't you send him back? Just for an hour or two?

PLUTO: What good would it do? It would only open a fresh wound and renew his pains.

* * *

XXIV

[DIOGENES. MAUSOLUS.]

DIOGENES: You really think you're better than the rest of us—don't you, Mausolus?

MAUSOLUS: Of course. I was a king—king of all Caria, ruler of many Lydians, subduer of islands, conqueror of nearly the whole of Ionia, even to the borders of Miletus. I was handsome, of noble stature, and a mighty warrior. My tomb is gigantic—of such dimensions, of such exquisite beauty as no other shade can boast. It was one of the Seven Wonders of the ancient world, and I defy you to name a temple to match it in magnificence. These are the grounds of my pride—are they inadequate?

DIOGENES: Kingship, beauty, heavy tomb ... is that it?

MAUSOLUS: Isn't that enough?

DIOGENES: But, my handsome Mausolus, your empire no longer exists. If we were to appoint an umpire now on the question of looks, I see no reason why he should prefer your skull to mine. Both are bald and bare of flesh—our teeth are equally visible—each of us has lost his eyes, and each is snub-nosed. As for your tomb, it too stands in ruins—its magnificence remains only in your memory.

MAUSOLUS: Then it was all for nothing? Mausolus and Diogenes are to rank as equals?

DIOGENES: Equals! Hah! I wouldn't say that! While Mausolus is groaning over his lost tomb, Diogenes knows not whether he has a tomb or no—the question never having occurred to him—he knows only that his name has come down through history as one who lived a life of wisdom—a higher monument than yours, vile Carian slave, and set on firmer foundations.

* * *

XXV

[NIREUS. THERSITES. MICHAEL MOORE.]

NIREUS: Here we are—this fellow shall award the palm of beauty.

MICHAEL MOORE: Who—me?

NIREUS: That's right. Now be honest—who's better looking? Me or him?

MICHAEL MOORE: Well, who are you? I should know that first—shouldn't I?

NIREUS: Nireus and Thersites.

MICHAEL MOORE: Which is which?

THERSITES: I'm Thersites—who Homer himself called the handsomest of men.

NIREUS: And I'm Nireus, the "Comeliest of all that came 'neath Trojan walls."

MICHAEL MOORE: Wait—wasn't Homer blind?

NIREUS: Still, he had excellent powers of perception.

MICHAEL MOORE: Well … your bones look about the same to me. The only difference I see is that your skull wouldn't take much to bash it in. It's a little thin—not very masculine.

NIREUS: Ask Homer what I was, when I sailed with the Achaeans.

MICHAEL MOORE: Dreams, dreams. I'm looking at what you are now—what you were is ancient history.

THERSITES: Accept his judgment, Nireus—he has found me handsomer of the two.

MICHAEL MOORE: That's not what I said. You're not handsome at all. Either of you. Or anyone else down here for that matter. Hades is a democracy—one man is as good as another here. Just a pile of bones.

* * *

XXVI

[MICHAEL MOORE. CHIRON.]

MICHAEL MOORE: Chiron! Is it true that you were a god, and that you actually chose to die?

CHIRON: It's true. I'm quite dead—and I could have been immortal if I'd wanted.

MICHAEL MOORE: Why did you do it? Death doesn't have much charm for most people.

CHIRON: You seem like a reasonable guy, so I'll tell you the truth—I was bored. There was no further satisfaction to be had from immortality.

MICHAEL MOORE: It wasn't satisfying just to be alive—to breathe the air and feel the sun on your face?

CHIRON: No. Variety is the spice of life, as they say, and I'd seen it all. I was only repeating myself. Life had become monotonous—there's no pleasure in that. Living on and on, everything always the same—sun, light, food, spring, summer, autumn, winter, one thing after the other in predictable sequence. I got sick of it. I discovered that continual possession of a thing does not lead to enjoyment—that deprivation is required too.

MICHAEL MOORE: Be careful, Chiron! You may be caught in the snare of your own reasoning.

CHIRON: How so?

MICHAEL MOORE: Well, if the monotony of the other world became tiresome, won't this one do the same? You'll have to look for another change, but I suspect you've reached the end of the line—there's no third life possible.

CHIRON: And what solution do you propose?

MICHAEL MOORE: Who said anything about a solution?

* * *

XXVII

[DIOGENES. ANTISTHENES. CRATES.]

DIOGENES: Hey, guys—want to take a stroll over to the entrance and check out the new arrivals?

ANTISTHENES: It might be amusing.

CRATES: Yeah. It's always fun to watch grown men weeping and crying for their mommies.

ANTISTHENES: My favorite is when they resist—when Hermes collars them and they dig their heels in and throw their weight back like stubborn dogs—as if it could do any good!

CRATES: Have I ever told you about my arrival?

DIOGENES: I don't think so. If you did, I don't remember.

CRATES: We were a large party. The most distinguished among us were Ismenodorus, a rich townsman of ours, and Arsaces, ruler of Media. Ismenodorus had been murdered by robbers on his way to Eleusis, by way of Cithaeron, I think. He was moaning and carrying on about his wound and the young children he'd left behind. Kept cursing himself for a fool. He knew the Cithaeron and the Eleutherae districts had been devastated by the wars, you know, overrun by thieves and all that, but he took only two servants with him to guard a whole carriage full of gold—the thieves were laughing at his stupidity when they killed him.

DIOGENES: What about the other fellow?

CRATES: Arsaces was an old man, rather imposing. He expressed his feelings in true barbaric fashion—grunted a lot, turned red in the face. He was really ticked off about having to walk and kept calling for his horse. As it turns out, his horse had died with him—the two of them simultaneously transfixed by a Thracian pikeman.

ANTISTHENES: Simultaneously? How is that possible?

CRATES: Oh, quite simple. The old goat was charging with his thirty-foot lance in front of him—the Thracian knocked it aside with his buckler and knelt, receiving the charge on his pike which pierced the horse's chest—the spirited beast impaling itself by its own force— and finally ran Arsaces through groin and buttocks! A Median shish kebob—man, horse and all! When he told us, I laughed my ass off!

DIOGENES: Here we are at the gate. Keep your eyes open.

ANTISTHENES: It's a mixed crowd today. All in tears except the newborns.

CRATES: Even the oldest and most arthritic are crying like babies.

DIOGENES: I'll interrogate this most reverend senior of them all. Excuse me! Sir! Why do you weep? You obviously enjoyed a long life. Were you a king, perhaps, and sorry to leave your kingdom behind?

PAUPER: No—I was no king.

DIOGENES: A provincial governor, then?

PAUPER: No. Not that either.

DIOGENES: Well, you must have been wealthy—how much gold did you leave unspent?

PAUPER: You don't understand. I was a fisherman—lived hand to mouth. I never had any money. I was childless, a cripple, and almost blind.

DIOGENES: And you still wanted to live?

PAUPER: Yes! Sweet is the light, and dread is death!

DIOGENES: I don't understand you, old man. At your age, I would have thought you'd be begging for death as the cure for all your ills.

PAUPER: Never! I'd live forever if I could!

ANTISTHENES: We'd better be on our way, Diogenes, before our loitering causes suspicion—they may think we are planning an escape.

PAUPER: Escape! Is that possible?!

DIOGENES: Don't get your hopes up, old man. It's never happened yet.

* * *

XXVIII

[MICHAEL MOORE. TIRESIAS.]

MICHAEL MOORE: So, Tiresias, I've been reading up on my mythology, and I found an interesting bit of trivia.

TIRESIAS: What's that?

MICHAEL MOORE: That you enjoy the unique distinction of having been both man and woman. I'm curious, how does that work and which life did you find more pleasant—the man's or the woman's?

TIRESIAS: The woman's—no question.

MICHAEL MOORE: Really?

TIRESIAS: Oh, yes—it was much less trouble. Women always rule the house; and there's no fighting for them, no manning of walls, no squabbling in the assembly, no cross-examination in the law-courts.

MICHAEL MOORE: That may have been true during your day, but in my time women have all the same responsibilities as men—plus they still have the whole pain of childbirth thing.

TIRESIAS: Then I may have to reconsider my answer.

MICHAEL MOORE: Did you ever have a child when you were a woman?

TIRESIAS: No. Thank god.

MICHAEL MOORE: But you could have—if you'd wanted to?

TIRESIAS: I suppose I could have.

MICHAEL MOORE: And your feminine characteristics just gradually vanished—you slowly developed a beard and became a man again? Or did the change take place in an instant?

TIRESIAS: You don't believe me? You think I made the whole thing up?

MICHAEL MOORE: Let's just say I'm skeptical. Do you really expect me to accept that story without asking any questions?

TIRESIAS: Are you equally skeptical when you hear tales of women turned into birds or trees or beasts—Aedon for instance, or Daphne, or Callisto?

MICHAEL MOORE: If I run across any of those chicks, I'll see what they have to say about it. But back to you—were you a prophet even in the days of your femininity? Or did manhood and prophecy come together?

TIRESIAS: Pooh! You're just making fun of me now!

MICHAEL MOORE: I just don't trust you. You're a prophet, and prophets lie—it's in their nature.

* * *

XXIX

[AGAMEMNON. AJAX.]

AGAMEMNON: You went mad, Ajax! You brought about your own destruction! How can you blame Odysseus?

AJAX: If I went mad, it was the Ithacan's fault! He cheated me out of my inheritance!

AGAMEMNON: Did you really expect him to let you have it without a contest?

AJAX: The armor was mine by natural right! I was Achilles' cousin! The rest of you recognized that—only Odysseus challenged me for the prize! Do you know how many times I rescued that ungrateful bastard in battle?! He would have been cut to pieces by the Phrygians if not for me. And yet he dared to claim himself a better man than me!

AGAMEMNON: If you want to blame someone, perhaps you should blame Thetis—she was the one who, instead of delivering the inheritance to the next of kin, left the ownership an open question.

AJAX: No, no; the guilt was in claiming them—alone, I mean.

AGAMEMNON: Surely, Ajax, you can forgive Odysseus for the sin of coveting honor. We all did, after all—that's why we became adventurers.

AJAX: You ask too much, Agamemnon. I cannot cease to hate Odysseus. It's not in my power—even if Athena herself should require it of me.

* * *

XXX

[PLUTO. JACK THE RIPPER.]

PLUTO: Jack the Ripper. I've been looking forward to this. Hermes, take Jack here, and drop him into the Pyriphlegethon.

JACK THE RIPPER: The Pyriphlegethon? What's that?

PLUTO: Oh, it's a river of fire. We keep it nice and hot for the likes of you. You'll be quite uncomfortable, I promise you that. And if you get accustomed to the pain, we have plenty of other tortures devised for your enjoyment. We can lay you alongside Tityus to have your liver torn by vultures or leave you to the claws of the Chimera. Get him out of my sight.

JACK THE RIPPER: One word before I go.

PLUTO: You dare to beg for mercy? After the things you've done?

JACK THE RIPPER: I don't deny my crimes. I only ask you to consider whether my sentence is just.

PLUTO: Whether it's *just?!* I only wish I had more tortures to saddle you with!

JACK THE RIPPER: Well, do you mind answering a few questions? It won't take a minute.

PLUTO: Talk quickly—before I lose my patience.

JACK THE RIPPER: My crimes—were they my own choice, or were they decreed by Fate?

PLUTO: Decreed, of course.

JACK THE RIPPER: Then all of us, whether we passed for honest men or murderers, were the instruments of Fate in everything we did?

PLUTO: Certainly; Clotho prescribes the conduct of every man at his birth.

JACK THE RIPPER: Now suppose a man commits a murder under compulsion of a power which he cannot resist—an executioner, a commanding officer, or a tyrant. Who is the murderer, in your opinion?

PLUTO: The officer, of course, or the tyrant. You might as well ask whether the sword is guilty, which is but the tool of the murderer.

JACK THE RIPPER: Thanks—I hadn't thought of that particular analogy. I'm indebted to you for a further illustration of my argument.

PLUTO: Get on with it.

JACK THE RIPPER: All right. A slave is sent by his master to bring me gold or silver—who should I be grateful to? The slave or the master?

PLUTO: The sender—the slave is but the minister of his master's will.

JACK THE RIPPER: Observe then your injustice! You punish those of us who are but slaves to Clotho's whims and reward others who merely administer his generosity. I didn't choose to be a villain—but it was not in my power to resist the irresistible ordinances of Fate.

PLUTO: Ah, Jack—if you look closely, you'll find more injustices than this. I see you are no common murderer, but a philosopher in your own way. Let him go, Hermes—I can't punish him after that. But listen, Jack, keep this to yourself—you mustn't put ideas like this into other people's heads.

* * *